Picture Day

More
Super ♡ Duper ♡ Royal ♡ Deluxe
books!

Missy's
Super ♥ Duper ♥ Royal ♥ Deluxe

Picture Day
By
Susan Nees

BRANCHES
SCHOLASTIC INC.

For Jeanette and Kenneth

No part of this work may be reproduced, stored in a retrieval system, or transmitted in any form or by any means, electronic, mechanical, photocopying, recording, or otherwise, without written permission of the publisher. For information regarding permission, write to Scholastic Inc., Attention: Permissions Department, 557 Broadway, New York, NY 10012.

Library of Congress Cataloging-in-Publication Data

Nees, Susan.
Picture day / by Susan Nees.
p. cm. -- (Missy's super duper royal deluxe ; 1)
Summary: After her mother helps with her outfit, Missy is afraid her school picture will not be special this year.
ISBN 978-0-545-43851-3 (pbk.)
[1. Clothing and dress--Fiction. 2. Photography--Fiction. 3.Schools--Fiction.] I. Title.
PZ7.N384Pic 2012
[E]--dc23

2011041464

ISBN 978-0-545-49609-4 (hardcover) / ISBN 978-0-545-43851-3 (paperback)

Copyright © 2013 by Susan Nees

16 15 14 13 12 11 10 9   15 16 17 18 19/0

Printed in China   38
First Scholastic printing, May 2013

Table of Contents

Chapter One
Missy

This is Melissa Abigail Rose.

But everyone calls her "Missy."

This is Missy's cat Pink.

Everyone calls him "Pink."

Missy keeps a journal. It is under her bed—along with one squashed bug, a bubble gum wrapper, three dirty socks, and last year's science project.

Missy keeps very important notes in
her journal.

Missy

What I LOVE!!!
horses
plaid
jumping rope
secret spying
glitter
cowboy boots
race cars
bubble baths

Pink

What I DO not LOVE!!!
alarm clocks
cleaning my room
table manners
sardines
kitty chores
homework

Mornings are especially busy for Missy.
Every morning before school, Missy has
to feed Pink and eat breakfast.

After breakfast, Missy has to get dressed.
Missy loves getting dressed. But it takes
her forever.

Missy does not just get dressed.
She gets dressed and jumps rope—
over and over and over again!

Miss Mary
Mack Mack Mack,

all dressed in
black black black,

had silver
buttons buttons buttons,

all down her
back back back...

Missy's cat Pink likes getting dressed, too...

Now don't be silly, Pink, you know it's time to get dressed.

MEEOOOOOWwww

...but not as much as Missy.

Chapter Two

Super Duper Royal Deluxe

Missy could not wait until Friday. Friday was picture day at school. And Missy was going to dress up Super Duper Royal Deluxe. She was going to razzle and dazzle! She was going to shimmer and shine!

Missy thought about picture day morning, noon, and night. On Wednesday, Missy thought about it while she was...

making her bed...

eating her dinner...

and doing her homework.

She even thought about it in the bathtub.

RINGS

HEARTS

RUFFLES

TIGHTS

PLAID

STARS

BOOTS

BLING

RAINBOWS

On Thursday night, just
before falling asleep,
Missy thought about it some
more. She thought about
belts that glitter,
tights with stripes,
and shoes that shine.

On Friday morning, Missy woke up bright and early. Picture day was finally here!

Missy went right to work. There was not a second to waste.

Missy mixed and matched. She belted and buckled. Today was THE day to dress up Super Duper Royal Deluxe!

Needs more ruffles.

Hello, world!

Beach-errific!

Does this need goggles?

Cha-cha-cha!

Think adventure.

Love it.

Super
Duper!

Styling!

Bling-a-zing!

Uptown
girl.

Dy-na-mite!

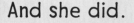

And she did.

DAISY PIN

SUPER DUPER FUZZY HAT

MR. NIBBLES

GLOW-IN-THE-DARK RING

HEART BUCKLE

SPARKLY BAG

PLAID
(NEVER LEAVE HOME WITHOUT IT!)

DYNAMITE BOOTS

Missy's mother took one look at Missy's outfit and said, "Goodness gracious!" Missy's mother decided that Missy needed help with her picture day outfit.

Today of all days, Missy did not need any help. And Missy did not want any help.

Missy's picture day was completely, totally, absolutely...

Chapter Three

No Ruffles, No Rainbows, No Ribbons, No Sparkles, No Nothing!

On the way to school, Missy did not want to sit with anyone. She sat all by herself and grumbled. Everything was ruined!

At school, Missy did not want to talk to anyone. And she did not want anyone to talk to her.

During Social Studies, Missy sat next to Oscar. She knew Oscar was not a talker. Oscar was a thinker.

Oscar looked at Missy. Missy was right.
Her outfit had no ruffles, rainbows, ribbons,
or sparkles.

But then, Oscar saw something else. He saw something better than ruffles, rainbows, ribbons, and sparkles.

Missy's teacher, Miss Snodgrass, was making her rounds.

Later that morning, Missy still did not feel like talking to anyone. She did not feel like talking to anyone, that is, except Oscar.

During Math, Missy was in no mood to listen to Miss Snodgrass. She looked around the room and sighed.

Everywhere she looked, she saw ruffles,
rainbows, ribbons, and sparkles.

At lunch, Missy sat next to Oscar again.

Oscar had to think fast.

Just then, the bell rang.

It was time—picture time.

Chapter Four
Say "Cheese" Please

Now I know you are all very excited about picture day, but we have rules and ... blah, blah, blah ...

Miss Snodgrass called for Room 916 to line up. She told everyone to smile and say "cheese" when they got their pictures taken.

Miss Snodgrass went on to remind everyone how to behave like young ladies and gentlemen.

Don't run, climb, jump, jog, shimmy, shake, twirl, wiggle, wag, clap, slap, rap, nap, hop, or skip. Don't yell, holler, growl, or bark. Don't crowd, don't pinch, don't... blah, blah, blah...

The students all went to take their places in line.

Missy did not want to line up or say "cheese." And smiling? Forget it! Smiling was the last thing she wanted to do.

Today was turning out to be Missy's worst picture day EVER. And it was about to get worse.

First, my picture day outfit is ruined. Then my day is super duper bad. And then after that you won't share your chocolate pudding, and now—

Miss Snodgrass pulled Missy and Oscar out of line.

Listen up, you two— Now, I realize you both are very excited about your school pictures. However, you still need to behave. Remember: No yelling, shouting, hollering, howling, blah, blah, blah…

Chapter Five

Oscar the Thinker

Miss Snodgrass sat Missy and Oscar down on a bench. She told them to wait. They would have to wait until everyone else had finished getting their pictures taken. Then it would be their turn.

So Missy and Oscar sat. They watched as, one by one, their classmates got their pictures taken.

Paulette

Benjamin

Alice

Emma Rose

Taylor

Henry

Lily

Dexter

Samuel

Nina and Nona

Josey

They waited and waited. And waited!

Oscar was beginning to wonder if this *was* such a great idea.

Chapter Six

Picture Perfect

The rest of the students had all filed past Missy and Oscar's bench. They had all posed for the camera, smiled, and said "cheese." It was finally picture time for Missy and Oscar.

Missy and Oscar were ready. In fact, they were so ready, they were already smiling.

That Oscar! He did know about plaid and friends and sharing after all.

And if there was one thing
Melissa Abigail Rose
really did know about,
it was dressing up—

Super Duper Royal Deluxe!

The End

Susan Nees

lives in Georgia with her family, a dog named Jodo, and a small flock of chickens. Although Susan always had to wear a plaid pleated uniform to school, picture day was the one day that she could dress up. She remembers a second-grade photo with a certain super duper hairdo. This hairdo was fondly named "the bird's nest" and it required glittery pink Dippity-do hair gel, and a satin bow.